SAM and CHARLIE (AND SAM TOO) HELP SAVE the EARTH!

Leslie Kimmelman

Illustrated by Jo Anne Davies

To Lois, who does more than her
part to save the Earth—LK

For garden helpers
Darren and Georgia—JAD

Library of Congress Cataloging-in-Publication data
is on file with the publisher.

Illustrations by Jo Anne Davies
First published in the United States of America in 2021
by Albert Whitman & Company
ISBN 978-0-8075-7198-9 (paperback)

Printed in China

10 9 8 7 6 5 4 3 2 1 WKT 24 23 22 21 20

052131.2K1/B1652/A5

Design by Valerie Hernández

For more information about Albert Whitman & Company,
visit our website at www.albertwhitman.com.

SAM and CHARLIE (AND SAM TOO) HELP SAVE the EARTH!

Leslie Kimmelman *Illustrated by* Jo Anne Davies

Albert Whitman & Company
Chicago, Illinois

TABLE OF CONTENTS

"What you do makes a difference, and you have to decide what kind of difference you want to make."

—Jane Goodall

This is Sam.

This is Charlie, his next-door neighbor and fellow friend to Earth.

This is Charlie's little sister. Her name is Sam Too.

And who is this? Read this book and find out!

BIG LITTLE NEWS

Something big was going on at Sam's house.

"Something *gigantic*," Sam told his best friend Charlie. "Gigantic, but also tiny. Meet Leo, my new baby brother. He came a long way to be part of our family."

Sam, Charlie, and Charlie's little sister, Sam Too, looked in the crib.

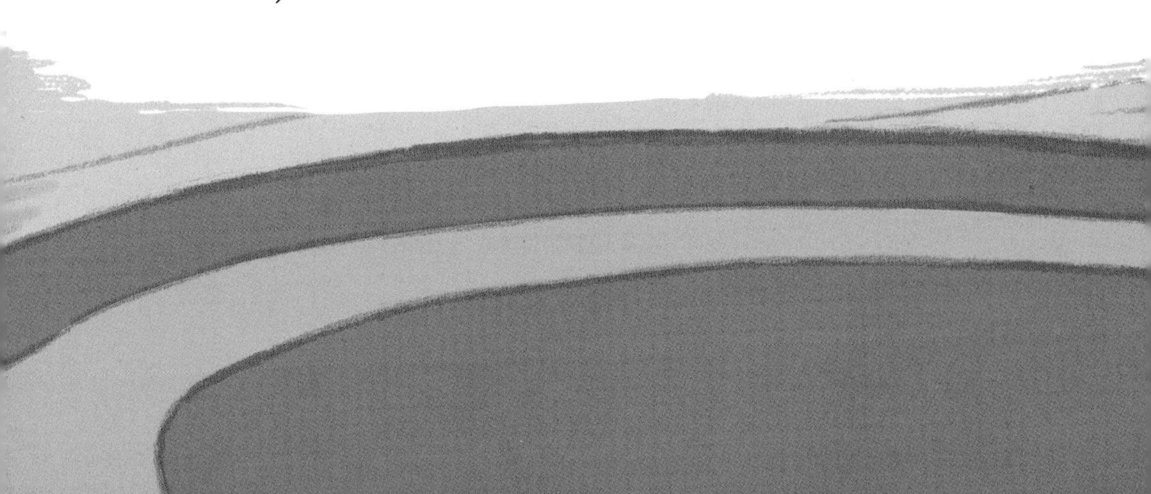

Leo looked back. Then he reached out his hand and grabbed Charlie's hair.

Sam held his breath. Charlie could be funny about her hair.

But Charlie smiled. "You are so smart, Leo. My hair is my secret weapon. It may *look* messy, but it holds all my power."

The next day, Sam's family planted a tree for Leo. It was a Jewish tradition. Everyone took turns watering the tree.

"Grow strong and tall," said Sam.

"Be green and shady," said Charlie.

"Welcome birds and rabbits," said Sam Too.

Everyone sat by the Leo tree. It was too small to give shade on hot days and too small for birds to nest in. "This tree will grow, just like Leo," Sam said.

"Everybody say *tree*," said Sam's mom. As she snapped a photo, Leo grabbed Charlie's hair with one hand. He grabbed Sam Too's hat with the other.

But he saved his smile for Sam.

“We need to keep the world green for Leo,” announced Sam the next night. “Right now our planet is in trouble. There’s a lot of work to do.”

What can three kids do to help the planet? thought Charlie.

"I've got it!" she said. She flicked the light switch to OFF. "Turning off lights saves electricity."

Whoa! It was pitch black.

"BOO!" yelled Sam, jumping out at Charlie and Sam Too. He tripped over a shoe and fell on his face.

"Nice try," said Charlie. "But not scary."

Sam sighed. "We can ride bikes more," he suggested. "Bikes use pedal power, not gas. They help keep the air clean."

"We can have a bike parade!" Charlie said.

"With signs!" added Sam Too. She loved parades.

They invited the whole street.

"Everyone will see that riding bikes is fun," Sam said. "*And* good for the planet."

Charlie and Sam Too wore brand-new bike helmets. Well, sort of brand-new.

"Charlene Olivia!" shouted a voice from

the crowd. “Samantha Rose!”

Charlie and Sam Too hated it when their mother used their full names.

“What have you done to your helmets?” she asked.

“We’re Earth heads,” answered Charlie. “No matter where we go, our brains are swirling with Earth thoughts. Earth is all around us.”

LOVE YOUR MOTHER
BE KIND TO EARTH
WHEELS FOR THE WORLD

TEN GOOD RULES

Sam Too finished her second cheese blintz and licked her fingers.

"Shavuot is delicious!" she said.

"Shavuot isn't just about blintzes," Sam's father replied, though it was true that his blintzes *were* the best. "It's also about the Ten Commandments, which God gave the Jewish people."

"Commandments are like rules," Charlie explained to her little sister. "Like 'Don't lie,' 'Don't steal,' and all that stuff."

"Don't forget 'Respect your parents,'" added Sam's father.

"I think it's time for ten *extra* commandments," said Sam. "For saving the Earth."

Everyone agreed that new commandments were a good idea. Sam got a big piece of paper.

Leo dropped a napkin on the floor.

"Great idea, Leo," said Charlie. She started a list:

1. DON'T LITTER

They had lots of good ideas.

2. RIDE YOUR BIKE

3. BE KIND TO ALL LIVING THINGS—NO SQUISHING BUGS (EXCEPT MOSQUITOES)

4. DON'T WASTE WATER (TAKE SHORT SHOWERS)

5. TAKE REUSABLE BAGS TO THE GROCERY STORE

6. TURN OFF LIGHTS

7. GROW A GARDEN

8. USE REFILLABLE WATER BOTTLES

Sam added a little drawing after each commandment.

There was no room for numbers nine and ten.

9. USE BOTH SIDES OF THE PAPER

1. Don't litter

2. Ride your bike

3. Be kind to all living things
No squishing bugs (except mosquitoes)

4. Don't waste water
(take short showers)

5. Take reusable bags to the grocery store

6. Turn off lights

7. Grow a garden

8. Use refillable water bottles

9. use both sides of the paper

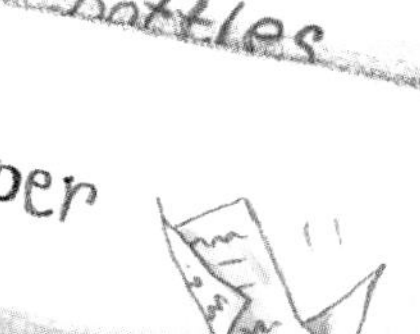

It was hard to think of number ten.
"**BLINTZES EVERY DAY!**" said Sam Too.

Ten extra-good *extra* rules.

OH JERUSALEM!

There was a gigantic pile of boxes in Sam's bedroom.

"From Leo's baby gifts," Sam said.

"Put them in the recycling pile," said

Sam Too. "Recycling helps keep the Earth clean and green. Something new gets made from something old."

“First, let’s *reuse* the boxes,” Charlie suggested. “That’s Earth-friendly too. We can build a tower.”

"Lots of towers," added Sam Too. "A whole city."

"Let's build Jerusalem!" said Sam, who had gone to Israel with his family the month before.

Jerusalem was awesome.

But with Leo in the house, the towers soon came tumbling down!

FINISHING THE SUKKAH

Summer was over. But Sam's favorite holiday, Sukkot, was just beginning. His mom and dad built a *sukkah*—a little hut—in the back yard. They piled branches

on the roof. They dragged the picnic table inside for eating meals. The sukkah *looked* finished, but…

"Something's missing," said Sam.

So he and Charlie and Sam Too tied long pieces of yarn around some fruits and vegetables. Sam's mom hung them from the roof beams.

“Something’s missing,” said Charlie.

So she and Sam and Sam Too made a long, colorful paper chain to hang up.

“Something’s missing,” said Sam Too.

So Sam brought out a long sheet of paper. Sam and Charlie and Sam Too made a mural for the walls. Their picture showed Leo’s tree, the bike parade, a mountain of blintzes, and the city of Jerusalem.

Was anything still missing?

Leo pointed up through the branches over the sukkah.

"Sky!" said Sam. "Great idea, little bro."

So they added the sky. The sky was very blue. The Earth was very green. The picture was perfect.

And the meal was scrumptious.

THE END